CLEVER C

and the Case
of the Worries

Bob Hartman

Illustrated by Steve Brown

DAVID C COOK

transforming lives together

CLEVER CUB AND THE CASE OF THE WORRIES
Published by David C Cook
4050 Lee Vance Drive
Colorado Springs, CO 80918 U.S.A.

Integrity Music Limited, a Division of David C Cook
Brighton, East Sussex BN1 2RE, England

The graphic circle C logo is a registered trademark of David C Cook.

All Scripture paraphrases are based on the ESV® Bible (The Holy Bible, English
Standard Version®), copyright © 2001 by Crossway, a publishing ministry of
Good News Publishers. Used by permission. All rights reserved.

Library of Congress Control Number 2022935582
ISBN 978-0-8307-8468-4

© 2023 Bob Hartman
Illustrations by Steve Brown. Copyright © 2023 David C Cook

The Team: Laura Derico, Stephanie Bennett, Judy Gillispie, James Hershberger, Susan Murdock
Cover Design: James Hershberger
Cover Art: Steve Brown

Printed in China
First Edition 2023

1 2 3 4 5 6 7 8 9 10

061522

"Mama, I can't stop thinking," Clever Cub said.

"Thinking about what, little one?" Mama Bear asked.

3

"**LOTS** of things," Clever Cub said. "Like when the wind blows hard,
I think Skippy Squirrel's treehouse might fall down."
Clever Cub pulled on one ear. He did that sometimes when he was worried.

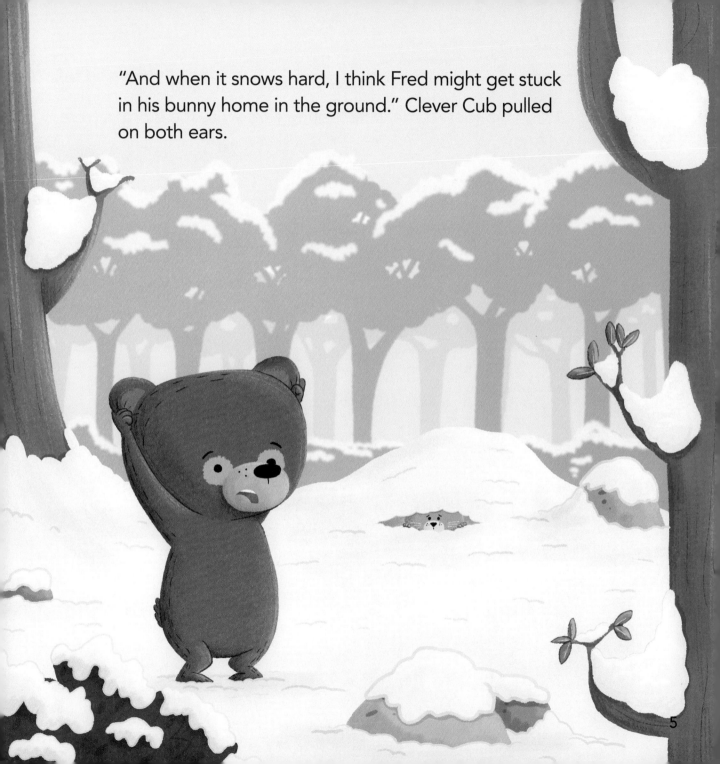

"And when it snows hard, I think Fred might get stuck in his bunny home in the ground." Clever Cub pulled on both ears.

5

"I see." Mama Bear nodded. "Sounds like you have a case of 'the **WORRIES**.'"

"I do?" Clever Cub wondered. He wasn't quite sure what the worries were. But it sounded **BAD**.

"And it sounds like you care about your friends **A LOT**."

"**YES**, I do," Clever Cub said. He was sure about that.

"And you don't want bad things to happen to them."

"**NO**, I don't!" Clever Cub stomped hard with each word. He was *very* sure about that!

"But have any of those bad things ever happened?" Mama Bear asked.

"No-o-o," Clever Cub said, shaking his head. Then he pulled on his ear again. "But they **MIGHT**!"

"Let's go for a walk up the mountain," Mama Bear said. "I have a story for you."

"A Bible story?" Clever Cub asked. He **LOVED** Bible stories.

"Good guess!" Mama Bear replied.

9

High up on the mountain, they looked down over the whole valley. Mama Bear found a warm, sunny spot to sit in and began her story. "One day Jesus sat down on the side of a mountain," she said. "A **BIG** crowd came to hear what He had to say."

10

"Jesus talked about how God **LOVES** us and wants us to take care of one another. Just like you care for your friends, Skippy and Fred." Mama Bear smiled at her cub. "But then Jesus looked out over that big crowd, and what do you think he saw?"

"A **MOOSE**?" Clever Cub waved to Old Marvin the moose, who was munching on a bit of shrubbery.

"No-o-o, not a moose." Mama Bear said. "I think he saw a worried look on some faces. I saw the same worried look on your face today."

"Did the people have the **WORRIES** too?" Clever Cub asked.

"Well ... maybe," Mama Bear said.

"What did Jesus tell them?" Clever Cub asked.

13

"He told the people to look up, up, **UP** in the air," Mama Bear said. Clever Cub looked up, up, up too. "What do you see?" Mama Bear asked.

"**BIRDS**!" Clever Cub shouted. "I see a flock of geese and some sparrows. And way up high, I see an eagle."

Mama Bear nodded. "Jesus asked the people a question: 'Do the birds of the air plant seeds in the ground and water them and watch them grow?'"

"That's a silly question!" Clever Cub chuckled. "Birds aren't **FARMERS**!"

"Exactly!" Mama Bear said, and she chuckled too. "But God makes sure all the birds have enough to eat. Jesus told the people not to worry about not having enough to eat. He said God would take care of them too."

Mama Bear continued. "Then Jesus told the people to look down, down, **DOWN** to the ground." Clever Cub got down on the ground and looked all around.

"What do you see?" Mama Bear asked.

"**FLOWERS**!" Clever Cub said. "I see a daisy and a buttercup and a dandelion."

"Lovely," Mama Bear said. "Jesus asked another question: 'Do the flowers make thread or sew fancy clothes to wear?'"

"That's a silly question too!" Clever Cub rolled on his back and giggled. "Flowers can't **SEW**!"

"Exactly!" Mama Bear said. "But God makes sure flowers look more beautiful than the richest king wearing the finest clothes. Jesus told the people not to worry about their clothes. He said, 'God will take care of you. You are more important than flowers.'"

Clever Cub said, "God takes care of the birds and the flowers. God takes care of **EVERYONE** and **EVERYTHING**!"

"That's right, my clever cub," said Mama Bear. "But Jesus asked the people one more question."

"What was it?" Clever Cub asked.

Mama Bear answered, "He asked them, 'Can you make your life last even an hour longer by worrying about it?'"

Clever Cub laughed loudly. "That's the silliest question of all! Of course **NOT**!"

Mama Bear laughed at her silly cub. "Exactly.
Having the worries doesn't change a thing.
It doesn't add hours to your life. It doesn't make
the wind stop blowing or the snow stop snowing.
It doesn't keep your friends safe. It's just a waste of **TIME**!"

"Exactly," Clever Cub said. He looked up, up, **UP** at the birds in the sky. He looked down, down, **DOWN** at the flowers on the ground. Then he looked all around and saw Old Marvin munching leaves and Skippy climbing a tree and Fred hopping up the hill.

Clever Cub scratched his nose. He did that when he was thinking. "Mama, do you ever get the **WORRIES**?" Clever Cub asked.

"Well … yes … sometimes," Mama Bear said. "But then I remember what Jesus said, and I know God will take care of me."

"And I know God will take care of me and my friends **TOO**!"
Clever Cub smiled. And then off he went,
down the mountain, with Fred and Skippy
and Old Marvin the moose.

23

For Clever Readers

Clever Cub is a curious little bear who **LOVES** to cuddle up with the Bible and learn about God! In this story, Clever Cub finds out he doesn't need to worry because God will take care of us all, just like Jesus said (Matthew 6:25–34) .

Have you ever had the worries? Did worrying make you feel better? We worry sometimes when we don't know what's going to happen. But God knows! We can depend on Him to take care of us. When you get worried, remember: God will take care of you!